Where The Journey Takes You

=======================
=================

Robert Eugene Perry

Published by Robert Eugene Perry

Please direct inquiries to REP Publishing
115 Main Street Oxford MA 01540

ISBN: 978-0-6151-4572-3
Printed in the United States of America

For my wife Kristina, without whose encouragement and inspiration this book would not have been completed.

And for Joshua and Zachary, who keep my spirit childlike.

I love you.

Contents

Prologue   1

Chapter I   The Calling   3

Chapter II   The Awakening   6

Chapter III   Trial by Fire   15

Chapter IV   The Joyful Healer   21

Chapter V   Whispery Voices   28

Chapter VI   The Cave   37

Chapter VII   Across the Ephemeral Plains   49

Chapter VIII   The Secret Language of Water   58

Chapter IX   Sacrifice Beneath the Stars   62

Chapter X   The Way to the Summit   69

Chapter XI   Catharsis   75

Chapter XII   The Riddle   80

Chapter XIII   A New Beginning   89

Epilogue   93

Cast of Characters   95

Prologue

Once there was a man who had a dream of what life was meant to be like. It was a lovely dream, full of the magic and color of heaven. All the things which appeared to him in this dream were exactly as they should be, and without judgment or bias he walked through his vision and was profoundly affected by all he took in.

As he walked through the ethereal garden of his fantasy, he discovered that although he was aware that he was dreaming, there was a certain sense of belonging which attached itself to him. He heard no words; all was conveyed through impressions, which brushed upon him like warm gusts of air.

Although he walked unaccompanied down the winding paths towards the distant shoreline, he did not feel alone. There was a tremendous sense of peace and communion with his surroundings. He felt as though he had been there all his life, and would continue his journey unencumbered by any anxieties or fears about his existence.

Upon awakening, he sprung out of bed in search of a pen and paper to write everything down. As it happens (which you will know if this has ever happened to you), by the time he found the things he was looking for, he had forgotten the details of the dream. He was, however, left with a strong sense of longing, and an unshakable belief in Something greater than himself.

Chapter I

The Calling

Jeremiah woke up with a start. He had fallen asleep with his head pressed against the cold glass of the Greyhound Bus window. He thought the tires must have hit a rut in the road, and he was now sitting bolt upright trying to gather his wits. The little girl in the seat across the aisle was watching him with interest. She was seated next to a middle aged woman who was fast asleep with a pillow between her head and the window.

"Did you know that you talk in your sleep?"

Jeremiah rubbed his eyes and turned to her. "I do? Really?"

She smiled with all the innocence of an eight year old. "Yes. You do."

He looked at his watch. It was three o'clock in the morning. "You should be sleeping like your Mom over there, I am fairly certain it must be past your bed time."

The little girl laughed. "What makes you think that this is my mom?"

Now Jeremiah was fully awake. "Isn't that your Mom? I just assumed, you know, a little girl sitting next to a middle aged woman traveling together on a Greyhound bus in the middle of the night. I used my powers of deductive reasoning." He thought he would have a bit of a fun teasing the girl, he waited for her to ask what deductive meant.

"What makes you think I'm a little girl? My size?" She looked at him with eyes that were filled with mirth. "You presume to know much, but for all your powers of deductive reasoning you clearly haven't the faintest idea what is going on."

The air felt different. He could feel the hairs on his arm tingling as they stood on end. "I'm sorry, what did you say?"

She looked at him again and laughed, a little girl laugh but with something behind her eyes like a treasured secret. "Don't you want to know what it was you were saying in your sleep? Or would you prefer some clever word play?" She began to sing:

"How would you address
a somnambulist?
would you lead him awake
with a fairy's kiss
would you dance in the dark
for his dreams to see
would he know who I am
when he looked at me?"

4

When she was done singing she looked at him expectantly. Jeremiah found it difficult to focus on his surroundings, everything around the girl was getting darker and she stood out as if she were made of light. "I don't…I don't understand…"

"Don't you remember? The field of clovers? Haven't you seen me before?"

There was a part of him that awakened at the sound of her voice.

"What is your name?" he whispered.

"Cassandra."

At the sound of her name, he felt himself sinking backwards into the seat, melting into a warm embrace, as he slowly began to awaken to his surroundings. The bus was still rumbling on through the night, the woman slept on in the seat across the aisle from him, and there was no sign of the little girl anywhere.

Chapter II

The Awakening

He looked at his watch. 3:33 AM. The scenery was still factories and refineries. The smoke which bellowed out of them seemed eerie in the artificial light of the city, like sleeping dragons letting their foul breath curl lazily around the buildings. Jeremiah sighed and took out his journal. He flipped on the overhead light and began writing:

Cassandra appeared in my dreams again. For some reason, I never recognize her until she says her name. It has been three months now since the first dream. I still don't know who she is, but in this dream she gave me a riddle rather than just leading me through places which seem hauntingly familiar. The only thing I remember is "somnambulist" and "fairy's kiss". I wonder how those words are related. Well, if she's a fairy then that explains everything about the dreams, but nothing about my journey. I wish that I could believe in the land of Faery, my heart longs for something more than what I can see around me. The move from pragmatist to romantic is a bit more involved than that though.

Jeremiah stopped writing and turned again to look out the window. The bus had finally moved through the cities and was now passing the maze of cornfields in search of their next destination. He breathed a little easier and began to relax as the bucolic setting and the motion of the bus rocked him back to sleep.

"Have you figured it out yet?"

Jeremiah was walking in a field of clovers, their bright green spread out in all directions as far as the eye could see. He looked over to see Cassandra walking next to him with that same radiant expression she always wore on her face.

"Why is it I remember that your name is Cassandra now? I never recognized you before until you spoke your name."

She smiled. "It was not time, I did not wish for you to know me. You are getting closer to your destination, your heart is reaching out towards me." She stopped abruptly and shot him a mischievous glance. "Have you thought about the riddle?"

Here in the confines of his sleep, he found it easy to recall the riddle. "Are you a fairy? A sprite? An elf?" He had felt a little foolish writing it in his journal, but here it felt a perfectly natural question to ask.

"I am all that and more", she answered. "You knew me once, but you are not yet ready to remember. Do not be afraid. You are never alone on your journey."

They were coming to the end of the field of clovers, there was a small cottage at the edge of a wood. Smoke drifted out of the top of the chimney, and there were sounds of hammering coming from the interior. Jeremiah turned to her, and she handed him a staff.

"No one should go on a journey without a walking stick. Keep it close by you at all times, it will help you in many ways as you travel along."

He took the staff from her and studied it. It was dark as ebony with a bone white handgrip at the top. All along the base were strange carvings which he could not decipher. "Cassandra, do the markings have meaning?"

"Indeed they do. You will find that their meaning will become clearer with the passage of time. You will also have need of this." She handed him a small flute, also ornately carved with strange runes.

"I'm sorry to disappoint you Cassandra, but I do not know how to play." Jeremiah cast a regretful look towards the ground.

"This is a special instrument, it already knows the music of the spirit. Carry it close to your heart, and play it when you feel the need to express something that words will not convey."

She held his hand for a moment and then gestured to the door. "Your journey begins here at the carpenter's hut. I must leave you now, but we will meet again soon. Don't forget to ask questions, it is how we learn," she stopped and gave him a knowing glance, "and how we become healed."

With those words she vanished in an array of colors, and Jeremiah found himself knocking on the door of the cottage.

"Come in, come in, no need to stand outside knocking," came a kindly voice from the other side of the door, "just remember to wipe your feet on the mat."

He looked down at the coarse mat under his feet. As he wiped his shoes, they began to break apart and dissolve into the fiber. He felt puzzled by the sense of release that accompanied the disintegration of his shoes, and as he opened the door he was greeted by an old man with a firm handshake.

"Welcome, young man, welcome!" he beamed. "Come inside and have a seat by the fire. I dare say Cassandra has lead you to my door, hmm?" He took Jeremiah gently by the arm and led him to a burnished chair by the fireside. "This is the guest's chair, please rest by the fire while I tend to the hospitality."

"Thank you kind sir," Jeremiah replied, "I feel that I am indebted to you. Is there something that I can help you with?" He felt as though he had entered an oasis in his weary life; just walking through the door of the cottage had been a balm on this difficult journey.

"No son, there will be time enough for you to help me later on. Just put your feet up on the footstool, and relax by the fire. You will find it easier to rest now that your shoes have been removed." He smiled in response to Jeremiah's questioning look; leaving him to ponder that cryptic statement, he walked into the adjoining room.

Jeremiah breathed in the odor of the cottage. It smelled of wood shavings, hot soup, and the fragrant wood burning in the fireplace. There was a mantle above the fire which appeared to be carved of one massive piece of mahogany. All along the front were gilded figures embossed upon the edge of the wood; the shadows from the fire played along the images and made then seem to come alive. There were scenes of knights rescuing maidens from the jaws of dragons, of wise men and women healing the sick, of travelers finding a safe haven, and of all sorts of mystical beasts: some good, some malign.

Turning his gaze from the enchanted mantle, he looked to the circular window facing the east. There was a fair amount of sun pouring in through the open window, and he knew it must be early in the day still, the sun herself had not risen higher than the trees outside the cottage. He could hear the birds whistling in the trees, and his soul was completely at peace with his surroundings.

"It has been a long time since I felt like this," he thought to himself. "I had almost forgotten what it was like to really breathe."

"Yes, yes, I am sure you are finding the atmosphere of the cottage to your liking?" The old man had reentered carrying a tray with two steaming silver mugs.

He handed one to Jeremiah, who gratefully took the mug from his host's weathered hands. He then turned and placed the tray on the worktable in the center of the room, pulled over a stool from the fireside, and sat down with his own cup directly across from Jeremiah.

Jeremiah inhaled the aroma of the warm brown liquid within the cup. It reminded him of coffee, cocoa, cinnamon, and peppermint all at the same time. His benefactor sat across from him and graced him with a smile that was like a warm embrace. As Jeremiah sipped the elixir he felt his strength renewed and his senses heightened.

"Please sir, would you tell me your name?"

"I am known as Bertram, young man."

"Have you lived here always?"

"For as long as I can remember."

Jeremiah looked into Bertram's face. There was no trace of judgment there. "Do you know of my journey?" he asked quietly.

"I know all about your journey, Jeremiah. The winds have borne your tale along to my ears. It is you, however, that I wish to hear about." He stopped and placed his hand gently on Jeremiah's, "It is you that I am concerned with. Why do you not speak your heart to me. You are safe here."

Jeremiah averted his eyes and looked at the fire. It had been many years since he had trusted anyone with his heart. Many years since he had trusted anyone at all. Part of him wanted to just make friendly conversation with Bertram, just to bask in the presence of someone who really cared. He fought the desire to let himself open up, instead he chose to let his focus stay on the fire.

Bertram continued to sit quietly, observing Jeremiah and nodding gently to himself as he sensed his guest's inner struggle. He sipped his own drink, then placed it on the floor in front of the fire. He stood slowly and reached for something on top of the mantle which looked like a globe of pure white stone. Then he sat down facing the fire with the globe cradled in both hands.

Jeremiah sipped his own cup and again had that feeling of heightened awareness. He looked over towards his host, who was now staring intently at the fire. The inner struggle became stronger, but his fears prevented him from speaking freely to Bertram. Jeremiah closed his eyes, and he heard a low, soft song begin to fill the cottage:

"In days of old, the knights came round
To slay the wicked dragons down
The captives freed, the maidens fair
Would sing their praises everywhere

They'd feast on meat and wine and bread
And toast the awful Dragon's head
Then off to dream about the Grail
They'd wake the morning, setting sail

The knights are gone, their legends left
within our hearts, yet sore bereft
are we who struggle with our plight
to see the world in black and white."

Bertram paused in his singing, looking over to find Jeremiah had covered his face and was gently weeping into his hands. He continued to weep softly, his tears sliding down his face and soaking the top of his garment. Bertram waited until the tears subsided and began to sing again, louder and more forcefully:

"O heart of stone that would be flesh
Surrender to Love's tender call
Cast aside life's vain pretense
Spend thyself, who would take all"

Jeremiah looked up, and was now transfixed by his host's presence. Bertram had stood up and was holding the stone globe aloft in his right hand, gesturing at the fire with the other. The flames rose higher and higher, seeming to undulate with the old man's gestures. The globe in his hand was no longer pure white, but was now marbled, and appeared more black than white.

"O prisoner of thine own desire
Cast thyself into the Fire
Be ye purged by selfless flame
Be ye now made whole again."

The air around Jeremiah was completely still, every nerve in his body tingled. He looked over at Bertram, who was now standing still as a statue gazing at the heavens. The globe had progressed from marbled to completely black. All of creation seemed to hang suspended, waiting for something to happen.

Jeremiah returned his attention to the fireplace. The fire itself seemed to reach out from the confines of the hearth with outstretched hands. He stood up slowly, knowing what he had to do.

"Forgive me..." he began, and fell to his knees.

The globe now began to change its shape. The old man looked down on Jeremiah and spoke gently, "May it be as you have said. You are forgiven."

The dark object in Bertram's hand now completed its transformation. The newly formed raven alit from Bertram's outstretched hand, circled three times around Jeremiah's head, and then flew out the circular window, crying out his mournful song for all to hear.

Bertram held out his hand to help Jeremiah up. He then handed him the staff the Cassandra had first given him outside the cottage. Bertram gave him a wise but sad smile and said, "You know what you need to do now, my son. Godspeed."

Somehow, Jeremiah knew exactly what he needed to do. He hesitated only a moment, and then abandoned all restraint and plunged headlong into the fire.

Chapter III

Trial by Fire

Cassandra was waiting for him when he emerged from the fireplace. The Greyhound was now rumbling down a lonely stretch of highway in the desert, the yellow sand and red rocks the only scenery for miles. There was no one else on the bus, even the driver seemed a phantasm as they sat next to each other near the back.

Jeremiah turned from the window slowly, absorbed in his thoughts. He was considering his experience in the fire, and trying to put together the questions that he wanted to ask Cassandra. When he turned to face her, he was startled to find that she had aged a good ten years, and was now a beautiful young woman.

She returned a smile for his bewildered stare. "You see me differently now because you yourself have changed. I am always the same, those who can see me will discover that I appear different to them as they progress in their own journeys. Is there something you wanted to ask me?"

Jeremiah felt his anxieties disappear as he looked into her deep blue eyes. They had lost some of their mischievous quality, which was replaced by a deep tranquility. Unsure of where to begin or how to ask, his thoughts turned to the flute inside his pocket. He took it out and looked at the strange lettering carved into the side. Most of the runes were still indecipherable, but he now understood the first word.

"Forgiveness..." he read aloud, and then put the flute to his lips and played.

The song that flowed from the instrument began as a slow melancholy tune, almost a funeral dirge. It seemed to originate from the deepest place of his being, plaintive and tinged with remorse. Cassandra sat expectantly, as the music seemed to envelop the two of them in a shroud of sorrow. Just when Jeremiah thought that his heart would break from the anguish, the melody began to change. It segued from the dour minor keys to a more hopeful strain, and he began to feel the weight of his burden lifting. He continued playing, all the while watching Cassandra as her expression became more and more animated.

Jeremiah closed his eyes and the music brought to mind his experience in the fire:

After diving into the fireplace, all thoughts were driven from his head except one: *surrender*. The raven had whispered that word into his ear as it circled about his head, and he knew that the only path towards healing was through the fire. Once inside the fireplace he discovered his clothes had burned away, but he was not the least bit singed. When he looked down at his body he noticed it was covered with golden scales which formed a type of gilded armor over his skin. He walked though the flames unharmed, seeking to find his way.

Off in the distance he could make out something moving through the fire. As it drew closer it seemed as if the inferno itself was coming alive, the flames twisting and writhing along the ground in a serpentine fashion.

All at once the conflagration shot towards the sky, and a great dragon appeared before him, born of the fire itself. Jeremiah stood frozen to the spot, gaping at the sudden appearance of the monster. Before he could react, the dragon opened wide its mouth and breathed out a foul smelling mixture of gas and flame.

As soon as the flames reached Jeremiah they sent him into a frenzy. The only thought that his mind would grab onto was the destruction of this vile beast. He used the only weapon at his disposal and rushed at the dragon with his staff.

He stabbed at it, beat on it, clubbed it, and tried to gouge its eyes out; but the dragon only continued to circle around him, breathing its toxic fumes and growing larger. He found that although the dragon's breath did not seem to damage him, every time it struck him he would go into another rage.

Jeremiah stopped to survey the situation. The dragon was so large now that it had to actually circle around itself to come back for an attack. Jeremiah fell down on his knees in the flames, and the anger slowly flowed out of him. The memory of his time in the cottage returned, Bertram's kindness and the raven's admonition came into clear focus in his mind's eye. He looked up and saw the dragon returning.

Jeremiah stood up and faced his attacker. "You have no power over me that I have not given to you. I will no longer fight you."

The creature once again spewed forth its vile breath and Jeremiah felt the rage flowing through his veins, but kept hold of the one word in his mind and allowed it to pass through him. The dragon continued for a time, but when it discovered that its victim would not retaliate it let out a roar of absolute fury and devoured Jeremiah on the spot.

****

"Do you understand the meaning of the vision?" Cassandra ventured.

Jeremiah had stopped playing the flute and came out of his reverie. The Greyhound was still rolling along through the desert, the shroud of sorrow that had covered them while he began playing had lifted, and the air seemed still and expectant.

"That is quite a flute," Jeremiah quipped. "Were you able to see the entire vision?" He had a feeling that she knew all about his experience even before he had started to play.

"I was there with you, Jeremiah."

Jeremiah pondered her statement. It always seemed that she spoke in layered meanings. "Do you mean that you were there with me just now when I played the flute, or where you there with me while I was in the fire?"

"Is there a difference? When you fell to your knees before the dragon, what is it that you thought of?"

"The cottage. The raven. Kindness...," he trailed off, waiting for her response.

"And while you were rushing at the beast, what filled your heart & mind?"

Jeremiah felt the rage rush back into his body and fought for control.

"Jeremiah," she spoke softly, "you have done well on this part of the journey. You have listened to your heart and surrendered your own will the best that you are able. As you now realize, the only way to destroy the dragon was to face it and allow it to pass through you. Learning to trust the wisdom of other people is always a painful reawakening." She took his hand in hers and gestured towards the back of the bus. "Come, there is someone I want you to meet."

They stood up together and walked the short distance to the back of the bus, stopping in front of the bathroom door. Jeremiah looked at her and could not suppress a laugh. "The bathroom? Who are we going to meet in the bathroom?"

Cassandra smiled at his good humor. "I would have thought by now you would have learned not to judge by appearances. Why don't you open the door and see for yourself?"

Jeremiah touched the handle. It felt warm to the touch, surprisingly soft and supple. He turned to speak to Cassandra and found that she had vanished again. He returned his attention to the door in front of him, and found that the doorknob had become the hand of a young woman. They were standing on the edge of a precipice, surrounded on all sides by the great sprawling desert, the Greyhound no longer in sight.

Chapter IV

The Joyful Healer

"My name is Gwendolen, Jeremiah. I am pleased to meet you. "

Jeremiah was momentarily taken aback by the change in his surroundings. The landscape was stark, but beautiful in its own desolate way. There were distant mesas and buttes colored with variegated reds, browns, and grays. The sky was a medley of colors; the setting sun had painted the stretched out clouds into a blazing array of crimson, deep blue, light pinks, and gold. Off in the distance he could make out a solitary black bird heading directly into the sunset.

Gwendolen observed the direction of his gaze. "He bears your burden to the West, Jeremiah."

Her voice snapped him out of his contemplation. "Is that the raven I met in Bertram's cottage? How far has he traveled? How far has he yet to go? I have felt so much lighter since entering Bertram's cottage. Do you know Bertram…oh, I'm so sorry, I missed your name…" Jeremiah stopped short, realizing he had been rambling on to someone he had only just met.

Gwendolen laughed, and her laughter was like the sound of rain falling on a dry land. "I have known the old healer for many years, I am a frequent guest in his cottage. I have mixed some of his most potent remedies myself," here she smiled and took Jeremiah's hands in hers. "The raven will bear that portion of your burden to the Land over the Sea. What he has taken is that which has prevented you from moving forward on your journey."

Jeremiah looked at her earnestly. "Why would he do that for me? I offered him nothing in return. I have nothing to give…"

"You may yet surprise yourself, Jeremiah. You have great potential, and that in itself is a tremendous gift. All life is sacred, and we have been imbued with two great gifts: the capacity to love, and the freedom to chose."

Jeremiah felt his heart stir within him. He could not doubt the sincerity of the woman who stood before him. She seemed to glow with confidence and unmitigated joy. He felt that he could follow her anywhere, that she would be a perfect companion on his journey, that she would certainly lead him straight to his destination without any missteps along the way.

"Gwendolen, are you to guide me for the remainder of my journey?"

She looked upon him with a gaze that was both kind and sympathetic. "I am honored that you hold such confidence in me Jeremiah, but you will have many guides throughout your journey. There is not one of us alone that can lead you to your destination."

Jeremiah's shoulders sagged and he looked out again at the barren landscape. The raven was now a tiny dot in the distance, Jeremiah wondered how far it was to the Land over the Sea where his burden was bound. The sun was nearly even with the horizon, and the evening shadows had begun to creep out onto the landscape.

Gwendolen turned and stood facing the wall of stone behind them and began to sing:

"The way is long, the path grows steep
where darkness gathers in the deep
yet we are children, born to light
we fear no shadows of the night

though many hours before we sleep
with constant vigilance we keep
the narrow path which leads the way
through Shadow's heart to greet the Day

the time has come, make swift our feet
Now! part the rock, and in we leap!"

The escarpment which they stood on began to tremble and shake as the wall of stone ripped apart from the center, revealing a well lit passageway into the heart of the mountain. Jeremiah looked incredulously from Gwendolen to the opening and then back again to Gwendolen.

She laughed, "I am stronger than I look, my friend."

Jeremiah smiled in return. "Apparently so." He walked over to the entrance and peered down the long steep entryway. "Are we taking this path through the mountain? I hope it is this well lit throughout; now that the evening is here there won't be any light at all, not even coming through the fissures and rifts in the mountainside."

"The mountain has its own light within, although there are many dark and twisted passageways that one could get lost in if he failed to be attentive in his journeying. Shall we enter?"

She led the way down the newly formed passage towards the heart of the mountain. Jeremiah followed using his staff to help walk along the roughly hewn steps which seemed to wind down forever into the very bowels of the earth. He marveled at the fact that Gwendolen seemed to glide effortlessly down the trail before him.

"Gwendolen, why is it that we need to go through the mountain? If I am bound for the Land over the Sea, wouldn't it make more sense to take the direct route through the desert?"

"You are not ready to face the night in the wasteland, Jeremiah, even with me as your guide. You must travel the path that is set before you. Each new experience builds on the one before. You cannot learn to build a house before you understand the working of each tool."

Presently she stopped at a small landing at the base of the rocky staircase they had been descending. Before them was a short rope bridge which spanned a deep chasm in the rock. The was no light whatsoever emanating out of the chasm, which accentuated the darkness even more.

"Gwendolen, where does the light come from? I do not see any source of illumination, natural or otherwise."

"The light emanates from the goodwill of the mountain itself, although you will find that some of the creatures here prefer the darkness, and so influence their surroundings accordingly."

Here she picked up a pebble from the ground and tossed it into the dark fissure before them. Jeremiah could hear the echo of the stone as it bounced off the walls on the way down, eventually making a distant 'plop' as it landed in a pool of liquid far below.

Gwendolen made a silencing gesture and pointed to the chasm. They stood side by side as a sound began to emerge from the depths beneath them. It began as a low hissing sound, and slowly began to get louder and more pronounced. Whatever the creatures were, there were many of them, and they appeared to be very agitated. The sound they produced made the hair on Jeremiah's arms stand on end.

"What…" Jeremiah began, but again Gwendolen put her finger to her lips and urged him to remain silent.

The hissing sounds turned to barely audible voices. Gwendolen touched Jeremiah's ears and the whispers became more pronounced.

"He is here."

"Has he come to join us?"

"We must tempt him."

The chorus of whispery voices swelled in assent.

"Does he know that we are here?"

"He will not recognize us when he sees us. We will use our cunning to beguile him. Who shall we send?"

There was a great deal of hissing and whispering, none of which was intelligible to Jeremiah. All at once, the voices fell silent.

"Then it is decided. I will go and prepare at once." The voices hissed their agreement and fell silent again.

Jeremiah looked up from the darkness and into the radiance of Gwendolen's face. "How do they know about me? What are they? How do I guard against them?" His heart began to beat very fast, he had not felt such fear since his journey began.

Gwendolen took him by the arm and led him over to sit upon a small stone bench which protruded from the wall. She then produced a small cordial from within the folds of her robes. She uncorked the bottle, and gave it to Jeremiah to drink. The aroma of the liquid within reminded him of his Grandmother's kitchen on Thanksgiving day, and as he closed his eyes and drank it he was momentarily transported back to those lighthearted days of his early childhood. Eventually Jeremiah's body began to relax, and Gwendolen took the empty bottle from his lax hand and replaced it within her vestments.

"Jeremiah, you must be on your guard against deception. There are those who would lead you astray with shallow praise and hollow promises. Be true to your heart's leading and you will do well. I must leave you for a time, but we will be reunited shortly. I promise you this: when you see me again, you will know me better and esteem me more dearly than you do now. Do not fear the unknown - trust your heart and remember to be grateful for all you have."

He opened his eyes and looked towards where her voice had been a moment before, and found that he was alone once again.

Chapter V

Whispery Voices

Jeremiah continued to sit on the bench for a time, trying to piece together Gwendolen's warning and attempting to figure out who the voices were and how best to prepare for whatever they had in store for him. Eventually, he decided the best course of action would be to move ahead and trust his intuition. The fear that had recently gripped him had vanished, leaving in its place a calm assurance.

He stood up and walked over to the chasm. There was no sound from below, and nothing to see except the strange darkness emanating from within, which seemed to swallow the light from all around the hole.

Jeremiah walked over to the rope bridge. It was about fifteen feet long, and appeared very secure. Once he began to cross the gap, he found the lighting changed the closer he came to the other side. Where on the way into the mountain everything seemed brightly illuminated, the deeper into the mountain he walked the dimmer the light appeared and the more pronounced the shadows became.

He stepped off the bridge and onto the other side. He found the rocks beneath his feet to be slippery, and used his staff to brace himself up against the rock wall. When he looked back towards the direction he had come, nothing at all was visible. The rope bridge seemed to vanish the moment he stepped off, leaving him no choice but to forge ahead.

There was enough light to walk by, but it was dim and provided only enough visibility to illumine the area immediately around his footsteps. The going was slow; the slick rocks and unsure footing made Jeremiah very conscious of every step. To his left was a sheer rock wall, which he used to brace himself when he became tired. He could not lean long against it, for it was covered with ice. The chill went right through to his very heart.

To the right of the path was a long fissure, perhaps part of that same chasm which he had crossed earlier. Whatever the case, he found that if he veered too close to the edge, the darkness seemed to overshadow him and sap his strength. After a time of struggling along this difficult passageway, he began to wonder why Gwendolen had left him, and if there was any point at all to following this path.

He found a large rock to sit down on, which was curiously shaped like a giant throne. As he sat and ruminated about his plight, he heard a sad, sweet song fill the air around him:

"O the suffering you have borne
unjust rejection, neglect and scorn
the weight of the world that you have worn
upon your weary shoulders

How you've earned a little rest
tried and tired, oft hard pressed
no one knows just how depressed
you feel as you get older.

Come with me, and take your ease
drink my tonic, you who grieve
I am someone who believes
in the victim they have made you

Lay your head now in my arms
I will keep you safe and warm
and shelter you from things that harm

and I will make you
the envy of all that hate you."

Jeremiah had been listening to the song fill the cavern, his former courage and confidence now replaced with a melancholy indifference to his surroundings, even in regards to his journey altogether. He sat lost in past memories of those who had wounded him, reliving the pain and giving in to thoughts of persecution and fantasies of retaliation.

The longer he sat, the more comfortable the rock became, and the more it seemed to mold to the contour of his body. After a while, the anger seemed to melt out of him, leaving only the sadness and thoughts of futility. It was almost as if the rock which now surrounded him absorbed his anger, and used it to fuel the molding process.

"Are you comfortable, Jeremiah?"

Jeremiah snapped out of his trance and stared wide-eyed at the woman before him. She was tall, thin, and austere. She had bright green eyes, a small pointed nose, tight set lips, and long black hair which was braided tightly together and hung down the length of the green silk kimono she wore. There was a cold beauty about her, and Jeremiah felt strangely comfortable in her presence, almost despite himself.

"Do I know you, madam?" he inquired.

"Not nearly as well as you should," she countered. "It comes from all this nonsense of running through fires and wandering around in caves. What on earth are you doing down here in this godforsaken mountain anyway?"

Jeremiah thought about her question for a moment. "This is the path that Gwendolen led me to. She told me that this was the way my journey must take me…"

"Right before she abandoned you to the treacherous passageways in this cold, dark mountain. Some guide she turned out to be," she spoke in a calm, even voice which dripped with false sincerity. "She left you all alone to fend for yourself. My poor Jeremiah, I would never leave you like that. She's just like all the others who have mistreated and abandoned you."

Jeremiah tried hard to recall the way he had felt when he was in Gwendolen's presence, and he could never remember having felt so alive before. How could that have been an illusion? He simply could not have been so mistaken about her. On the other hand, why did she say that she had to leave

31

him? He could not clearly recall the reason, and in his torpid state he had forgotten all about the whispery voices and Gwendolen's impassioned warning. The woman in front of him seemed to sense his inner turmoil, and pressed her point further.

"Yes, Jeremiah, she seemed so kind and thoughtful, but the truth is in our actions, isn't it? She led you down a dark and difficult path, and then let you slip and slide and freeze your way until I came to rescue you. Where would you be if not for me? You probably would have sat there in that chair and froze to death. Take this," she produced a vial of bright green liquid which was the exact color of her eyes. "This will restore you to your former self and we can leave this accursed mountain together."

There was an eagerness and hunger in her eyes which made Jeremiah stir uneasily in his seat. It was at that point he realized that the stone on which he had been resting now held him fast.

"What's going on? How did you trap me in this chair?"

"You don't seem to understand, Jeremiah. I had nothing to do with your entrapment. You got yourself stuck in that chair. All that self righteous anger oozed out of your pores and became the glue which holds you fixed in that spot. Why, if I hadn't come along when I did..."

"Who are you?" Jeremiah spat out. "How do I know that you are on my side? What's in the green vial? How did I end up in this place, anyway?" Jeremiah felt his anger returning, and eyed the staff which he had unfortunately left leaning against the cavern wall when he sat down.

The woman held him in her steady gaze, and continued speaking in the same mawkish tones. "Now, calm down Jeremiah, I have already told you that I came here to rescue you. I am not like those others, I do not expect anything of you. I know what a hard life you have had, how everyone has let you down and left you wounded. I will never abandon you. I am your one true friend. Just drink up this elixir, your bonds will be loosened and we can go back to the way things were before you started this foolish journey."

Something awoke in Jeremiah at the mention of his journey. "You would have me give up everything I have worked for in exchange for what? Your maudlin sympathy? Who are you, anyways? What is it that you are after?"

The woman gave him a pitying look. "What is it that *you* are after, Jeremiah? Did you really think that you could change who you are? Did you really suppose that those 'guides' of yours cared for your well being? Why do you think that they keep disappearing? Isn't it obvious? They are just playing a game with you, having a bit of fun at your expense. You can't possibly believe they care at all what happens to you. They think they are being charitable by giving you presents and false hope, but they don't know you like I do. My poor, misunderstood Jeremiah…"

Jeremiah finally reached the point where he could not tolerate this woman's coddling anymore. He sat up as straight as he could in his chair, looked her directly in the eyes, and shouted: "I DON'T WANT YOUR PITY!"

For the first time since she appeared, the woman lost her composure. She trembled slightly, and her voice lost some of its insipid quality as she continued:

"My dear Jeremiah, I will have you remember that it is *your* foolishness that has brought you to this reprehensible state. I would never have suggested that you go wandering around the countryside consorting with fairy creatures, or accepting strange brews mixed by curious old men, or wrestling with fiery dragons, or wandering around hopelessly lost in dark and dangerous caverns. Now look at you, hopelessly trapped in a stone throne of your own making. Let's be sensible now, drink this draft and we can go back to the life you and I shared so amiably. My goodness, there wasn't even a need to get off the bus!"

The mention of the bus returned his thoughts to Cassandra, and to the flute in his breast pocket. He had no way to reach either of the gifts that she had bestowed upon him, but his thoughts began to clear as he looked beyond the woman standing in front of him and focused instead on the staff he had left leaning against the wall. There, emblazoned against the black staff, some of the runes had changed and become legible. In bone white letters towards the top of the staff, Jeremiah read aloud:

"Gratitude…"

The woman gasped and staggered back into the wall. Her eyes grew big as saucers as she breathed out, "What did you say?"

Jeremiah regarded her reaction to this new word. He considered the implications, and then continued. "Why, I was just thinking about how grateful I was that I have had such wonderful guides along my journey. I would never have guessed that some of the things which hurt the most would teach me the most valuable lessons."

The woman looked on in absolute horror. Her whole appearance began to shift and become less defined. Jeremiah felt a song of thankfulness rising up from within him, and he closed his eyes and opened his mouth to let it forth.

"Through dark of night the Good will shine
and lead me towards the choicest vines
the decision mine, my will to yield
to the higher ground or the potter's field

I will rejoice, though all seems lost
I will give my all, and not count the cost
For no sacrifice can be called too grand
Now to chose the Good, and to make a
stand

O selfishness, my soul's foul bane
Depart from me, ne'er be seen again!"

Jeremiah finished his song and opened his eyes. There on the floor of the cavern where the woman had previously stood was a puddle of green slime oozing its way towards a crack in the cavern floor. It made strange whispery sounds as it slid into the crevice and out of sight.

Chapter VI

The Cave

Jeremiah breathed a sigh of relief at the departure of his unwelcome guest. He closed his eyes again and let the tension wash out of his body. His breathing slowed down, and he felt a calmness come over him. He let the time slip away, certain that he would hear Gwendolen's or Cassandra's voice at any minute.

His emotions began to shift from feeling grateful for the help that he had received, towards feeling pleased at his own cleverness in dispensing of the unpleasant woman. He began to fancy that he had managed to rid himself of her entirely on his own strength. He felt a powerful surge in his breast, and attempted to propel himself off the stone seat (to resume his journey), only to find that he was still stuck fast to the rock!

Jeremiah was astonished. He had been certain that in driving the woman away, his bonds would be loosed and he would be free to continue on his way. He also found himself angry over the fact that neither of his guides had bothered to show up and explain his current situation, or to lead him out of this mountain. In his indignation, he completely forgot the Word that had delivered him from the grip that the green eyed woman had upon him. He also forgot that it was precisely that self-righteous anger which had bound him to the stone in the first place.

He began to shout for Cassandra and Gwendolen. When they did not appear, he began to curse their apparent lack of concern for his welfare. The more he shouted, the darker the air around him became. He stopped shouting and began to quietly smolder, his anger seeping out of him and into the stone chair. He was so absorbed in his thoughts that he hardly noticed he was sinking until it was too late.

Jeremiah fell through the stone chair and landed in a slimy mud pit in a subterranean cavern. The sudden shock of the fall brought him back to his senses. He looked around and spied a dim light shimmering far off in the distance. The earlier luminescence that had helped him pick his way along the path was not to be found in this part of the mountain. He began slipping his way along, groping towards the distant flickering light.

His thoughts became gloomy and his mood continued to darken the farther he slogged his way through the strange viscous substance of the pit. It seemed to cling to him, forming a tight layer over his clothes and skin. To make matters worse, he did not have his staff to help pull him along. In his wretched state, he could not help allowing his anger to vent out of his mouth as he began to rant about everything that came to mind: beginning with his current situation and moving backwards over his life. In a short time he had covered his entire adulthood, bewailing the injuries he had sustained, both real and fancied. He was just beginning to move into the events of his adolescence when he came to the end of the pit.

"What next?" Jeremiah thought aloud as he dragged himself out and lay panting on the stone floor of the cavern. He propped himself up against the wall; he was certain now that the light he had been following was some type of fire, by the way it shimmered and reflected off the cavern walls. He looked down upon himself and saw that the stuff of the pit had attached itself to him like glue.

"Great," Jeremiah grumbled, "it looks like I've been tarred and feathered like some sort of outcast. I wonder what other surprises lie in store for me. I don't know what I was thinking when I agreed to this journey anyways."

Jeremiah felt a tingling sensation on his arms which ran all the way down his spine. His journey. It seemed like a million years ago since he sat in his Grandfather's kitchen, listening to the old man share his wisdom with his beloved grandson.

"Jeremiah," he said, "each of us has a purpose in the world. The Creator does not create without a purpose. The world is full of beauty, and it is full of pain. Part of our journey is to learn to appreciate the beauty, and to bring healing to those who suffer to soothe their pain."

"Like when you put a band-aid on my skinned knee, grampa?"

"Yes, just like that. Only there are many people in the world who suffer much deeper than that. There is only one thing that makes people better when they hurt inside."

"Do they have to swallow the band-aid to help their insides?"

The old man laughed gently at Jeremiah's innocence. "No, my boy, they need something that only we can give them. Something that does not come out of a box, but that comes from our hearts."

"What is it grampa?"

"Love and acceptance. The two great healers."

Jeremiah looked puzzled and his grandfather smiled and tousled his hair. "Someday you will understand. When you start your own journey, it will all begin to make sense. Don't be in too much of a hurry to grow up, okay?"

Jeremiah came out of his reflection and spoke aloud to himself - "Well, I certainly did take my time growing up, huh grampa?" He sighed. "I'm sorry I let you down. I haven't been real big on love and acceptance."

The turmoil within him continued to rage as he struggled to his feet. He knew that he should let go of the past which continued to haunt him and cause him misery and pain. At the same time, he could not let go of the anger and bitterness towards those who had caused him so much suffering.

He continued walking to the end of the corridor, feeling very self conscious about his appearance. As he turned the corner, the narrow pathway opened into a large underground room.

There in the middle of the stone floor was a large Frog-faced person, horrible to look at, but strangely fascinating. He was sitting cross-legged on the floor holding a stick and roasting some kind of meat over a small fire.

The walls of the cavern were hewn out into rough shelves, and on each of these shelves were large glass jars filled with noxious looking blobs of what appeared to be meat, just like the creature was cooking now.

Jeremiah walked over to the fire, and stood directly across from the creature. The Frog-man looked up from his cooking, and gave him a wide mouthed grin.

"How nice of you to dress up for dinner," he croaked out in a strange throaty voice. He laughed at the way Jeremiah winced, and then continued:

"Where have you come from boy?"

"I am on a journey, sir. Right now I am seeking the way out of this mountain. Can you help me?" Jeremiah had learned by this time not to judge by appearances, and hoped that this repulsive creature might, in fact, assist him in his quest.

The Frog-man studied him closely for a few minutes before he spoke. "Maybe…" he drawled, then let his tongue flick out of his mouth and snatch the meat on the end of his stick. As he began to chew, his skin became more frog-like and his eyes rolled back as he murmured, "Ah, sweet retribution…".

"I beg your pardon?" Jeremiah began to inquire.

"Just remembering old times, young friend." The Frog-man put down his stick and stood up facing Jeremiah. "Can I offer you something to eat?"

Jeremiah watched him walk over to the rows of jars. He fought hard to hide the revulsion he had experienced at watching this strange being eat its horrible dinner, and shuddered at the thought of partaking in the same manner.

"Do you know what really makes my blood boil?" he called over his shoulder as he walked over to the jars farthest away from the fire.

Not wishing to appear rude, Jeremiah opted to respond to the question rather than assume it was just rhetorical. "What is that, sir?"

"Self righteousness. When some people think that they are better than other people. I mean really," here he paused as he took down and examined a really nasty looking jar, "you would think by talking with *some* people that they actually believed themselves to be perfectly in the right all the time. That every choice they made was the right choice, and that when others choose a different path it is because they must be in error. I wonder if they are born with that arrogance, or if it is inherited. What say you, boy?"

Now Jeremiah had been observing the creature since it had eaten its meal and noticed some subtle changes in its appearance since he first came into the room. For one thing, it appeared less human, more amphibian. Uncertain of how to answer, he decided to respond to this question with one of his own.

"Well sir, I have always had a difficult time with confronting hypocrisy in other people. It has been suggested to me in the past that perhaps the thing which angers us the most about other people is the very thing we detest within ourselves. Do you think this might be true?"

The Frog-man chuckled as he approached Jeremiah. "Very clever, boy. I see that you have had some instruction along the way. I fear, however, that you are purposefully forgetting your own experiential knowledge. Need I remind you of the torment that you went through: the lies, the taunting, the humiliation, the abuse - do you want to excuse those things as something that is undesirable within yourself? I didn't think so. What they did is inexcusable. Unforgivable. And so we will continue to hate them, won't we Jeremiah?"

The creature had resumed its position on the floor while it was speaking, and had begun roasting the contents of this new jar over the fire. Jeremiah was completely stunned; he had not considered the impact that his past had impressed upon his present state of mind. The Frog-man was right, the anger and bitterness were there just lurking beneath the surface.

"All is not lost, my young friend. And things are not always as they appear. Can you deny that dark place within yourself? Does it not sometimes clamor for attention? Does it not cause us to sometimes act selfishly and curse our friends in time of doubt? Does it not cause us to fall and cover ourselves in shame?"

The Frog-man had been speaking in the same raspy voice, but his tone was surprisingly not reproachful, but rather empathetic. Jeremiah was surprised that he not only knew what had transpired right before he came into the cave, but that he seemed interested in what was going on with his journey. He was still not certain if the being before him was friend or foe, so he spoke cautiously.

"How shall I address you, sir? By what name are you called?"

"You are trying to determine my affiliation, boy. You want to know whether I am to assist you in your journey or to block your progress. Is this correct?"

Jeremiah thought it best at this point to be completely honest. "Yes, that is true."

"Well now, that is some refreshing honesty. You have had quite a journey so far, young man. You have made good choices and bad choices, you have moved forward and fallen back. And now you are here in this cavern, trying to make the right choice again. What is your desire? What is it that you have come here seeking? Is it simply to find a way out of this mountain, or is there something more?"

Jeremiah thought this over for a few minutes. Again, complete disclosure seemed the best course of action. "Healing, sir. I have come seeking healing. I have been wounded, and have embarked on this journey to get better."

"For what purpose?" the Frog-man asked.

"I'm sorry, what do you mean?"

"I mean," the Frog-man continued, "what is the purpose of your being healed?"

"I don't understand, sir. That is the purpose of my journey, the reason I was called in the first place."

"Oh, I don't think so. I believe that pain was the motivator, and that healing is what you seek to remove the pain. Once you are healed, what then?"

Jeremiah was taken aback. "I hadn't thought about that."

"I thought not. No matter," the Frog-man returned, "I appreciate your honesty. You asked my name, I shall give you some idea of who I am."

The creature then closed his eyes and sang in a voice quite unlike his hoarse speaking voice. It was plaintive and playful at the same time.

"It's funny how
It seems to be
That you're like you
And I'm like me
And that there is
No in-between
Or at least

That's what it seems

Can we look
Beyond the guise
And seek the truth
Behind the lies
Perhaps in time
We both will see
I'm quite like you
And you, like me."

His host had now finished his song and stood up, placing the stick in Jeremiah's hand.

"It is bitter going down, but it is sweet to the stomach," the Frog-man counseled. He put his hand upon Jeremiah's shoulder, and spoke softly – "the path to healing often takes unexpected turns. This one is part of your journey."

Jeremiah looked up from the ground and met the Frog-man's steady gaze. Beneath his grotesque exterior, his eyes were clear and bright and sincere. Jeremiah had no comprehension of the purpose of eating this foul offering, and was not exactly certain of his host's motives, but held onto one thing as certain: he had chosen to follow this journey regardless of any impediments and was acting in good faith. He closed his eyes and uttered a silent supplication for strength.

His first thought when the substance entered his mouth was how absolutely correct the Frog-man was. The bitterness was like poison to his tongue, and he had no choice but to chew it well, because it would not go down otherwise.

When he opened his eyes moments later, he found that the cave had disappeared and he was now in a long hallway. The floor was black marble; the ceiling translucent, with a sort of unearthly light shining through which illuminated the corridor as far as he could see. Each side of the corridor was lined with doors, and appeared to stretch out beyond the range of his vision. He could not, however, suppress the desire to look behind him; but found that when he did, everything appeared inverted.

When he looked behind him, it was he who was the Frog-man, and he was sitting alone by the fire roasting that same strange meat on a stick. It was like looking at something through the reverse end of a telescope, it appeared so small and far away. He had the most peculiar feeling watching himself by the fire, the Frog-man's soliloquy took on a new dimension in his thoughts as he turned once again to the passageway.

Jeremiah walked to the first door and peered through the glass pane in the top part. He saw a small child being bullied by a larger child. His chest tightened at the sight, this was a familiar enough experience from his own childhood. He put his hand to the doorknob to open the door and stop the aggressor, but drew his hand back quickly when he discovered it was hot as fire!

Jeremiah looked back through the window to see another scene. The bully was walking up the path of his own home. He no longer seemed intimidating, he walked slowly past the garbage strewn across the front yard. He looked up at the window with a face frozen in terror. Out of the house came an unkempt man with a can of beer in his hand, shouting something at the boy and making wild gestures. The boy looked like he wanted to turn and run, but thought better of it and walked up to the doorway. The man grabbed him by his shirt and roughly pulled him into the doorway and slammed it shut.

Jeremiah stood there stunned as the light in this doorway went out. He had never thought about the reasons why a person would want to intimidate someone else. He had been so locked into his own identity as victim that it had not occurred to him that everyone has their story, and that abusers could very well have been abused themselves.

As he turned from the doorway with this revelation in mind, all the other doors along the corridor began to fade from view. He started walking towards the end of the hallway, and discovered how light his step had become. He felt like skipping, but as he couldn't be sure that no one was watching (men don't like to be caught skipping or prancing, it is very undignified), he ran like the wind towards the far end. He ran for what seemed like miles, the doors disappearing before him as he ran, running solely for the joy of feeling unburdened and free from care. He laughed as he ran, and the sound rang out around him like the strains of a glorious chorus; till at last he came to the end of the hallway, where he burst out into an open field and threw himself down on the ground, still laughing, panting, and wondrously out of breath.

Chapter VII

Across the Ephemeral Plains

Jeremiah rested in the field for what seemed like hours, feeling the sun warm his face and staring at the bright blue sky. The release that he felt from leaving the mountain was palpable, and he had no desire to do anything but let his body relax and enjoy the sun.

After a time he heard the sound of music off in the distance. He experienced a sensation of absolute rapture, it was as if his heart had leapt out of his body and was dancing in the fields for the pure joy of being alive.

As the music became louder, he distinctly heard two voices joined in harmony. The voices seemed somewhat familiar, but the music they formed was altogether new to him. He could not separate the instruments from the singers; the music seemed to fill the air and envelop him in a warm embrace.

> "Acceptance brings
> the sweet release
> That hate denied

and grants us peace
To face ourselves
our pride aside
To give the love
we were denied

Wisdom's task
to show the way
When darkness shrouds
and doubt decays
To let us know
that feelings pass
Faith, hope, and love
are all that last

Joy will come
and pierce the pain
Letting life
come through again
Bringing truth
to all our sorrows
Exchanging despair
for bright tomorrows

The table placed
in pastures green
A banquet set
a lover's dream
The calling comes
for all who hear:
Accept the gift
refuse the fear.

While Jeremiah was watching the clouds roll
by overhead, Cassandra and Gwendolen came over

him, smiling and extending their hands to him. They lifted him up off the grass and greeted him with laughter and joyful embraces.

"I am so sorry that I doubted you," Jeremiah began.

"You ought to be ashamed of yourself," Gwendolen teased.

Cassandra laughed. "I think that he has exhibited sufficient remorse, Gwen." She stopped walking and looked searchingly into Jeremiah's eyes. "Did you find our melody uplifting, Jeremiah?"

Jeremiah tried to find the words to describe the way he was feeling. He had never experienced this type of elation before, he wanted to express both his gratitude and wonder at the changes that were occurring within him. When he looked up at Cassandra, he found that words were no longer necessary.

"You've aged another ten years. Have I been in the mountain that long?"

Cassandra smiled and returned his staff to him. "Not exactly. As I mentioned before..."

"Yes, that's right," returned Jeremiah. "You are always the same; it is my perception of you that has changed."

"Right as rain, my friend," Gwendolen interjected. She then pointed her finger towards the North. "Do you see that summit off in the distance?"

Jeremiah looked beyond the farther edge of the field they were walking on. He could see a distant path which wound its way up the hillside towards the apex of the mountain. He nodded his assent.

Gwendolen continued, "That is where we are bound. There is something that you will need to see from the vista at the top. Do you still have the flute in your pocket?"

"Yes, I do."

"Then take it out and play it. I think you will find that it adequately expresses the gratitude welling up in your heart."

He reached into his breast pocket and pulled out the small flute. Once again he looked at the carvings engraved there, and there was a second word that he could read, right next to forgiveness. This one appeared as: JOY.

He smiled as he placed the instrument once more to his lips and began to play. The melody which came forth was rich and strong, full of laughter and the joy of life. The troupe continued walking throughout the morning; they each took turns singing and playing music. Cassandra played a miniature harp and Gwendolen a small lute, which they each drew from the folds of their garments. They continued traveling along in joyful company, eventually arriving at an old stone bridge which spanned a swift moving river.

The water splashed and rolled over the stones; the three of them stopped to listen to the lively music the river was making. While they were enjoying the joyful sound of the stream, Jeremiah saw something swimming towards them just underneath the surface.

"What is that?" he asked Gwendolen.

"Well, what does it look like to you?" she returned.

Jeremiah observed the creature swimming towards them. The dark shadow was about the size of a person, but the form kept shifting and changing so it appeared that it was almost as fluid as the river itself. "It looks like a part of the river come to life."

Gwendolen and Cassandra both turned and beamed at him.

"Very astute, my friend," Cassandra encouraged. Then she called out to the rapidly approaching form, "Hail Shannon! We have brought a friend from a distant land in need of your guidance!"

Jeremiah was amazed when the water did indeed come to life. The creature which rose up out of the river was made entirely of the river itself. The sun sparkled and shone through its body, making it seem like it was bedecked with jewels from top to bottom. When Shannon spoke it was in a flowing, melodious voice, as if the river itself was speaking.

"Welcome Jeremiah. I am Shannon, the daughter of Old Man River. Perhaps you would care to accompany me for awhile; I can answer many of your questions."

Jeremiah turned to Cassandra, "Wasn't there something you wanted me to see from the top of the mountain?"

"There will be plenty of time for that later. You will have a better understanding if you spend some time with Shannon first. She will see to it that you meet us at the summit later."

"How can a river take me to the top of a mountain?" he asked.

Shannon laughed. "Come along and find out."

Gwendolen and Cassandra caught him up under the arms tossed him into the fast moving current. After the momentary shock wore off he realized he was lying on his back, and was now traveling on the back of Shannon herself. His companions were smiling and waving their goodbyes. He returned their farewell and then turned around to face the way they were journeying downstream.

The sensation of riding on the back of living water was exhilarating. Half of Jeremiah was below water; Shannon herself was flowing and changing below with the river, while her upper half remained constant above. Jeremiah could not feel anything below his waist, it was almost as if he and Shannon had merged and become one entity.

They flowed with the river for some time in silence. Jeremiah was taking in the sights and was amazed at how sharp his senses had become. He could smell all the different flowers that were growing along the riverbanks, and pick out each individual scent. All of the land seemed in complete harmony;

the creeping things, the flying creatures, the plants and trees: all appeared to be a part of an elaborate dance. He watched them in awe as his joy continued to overflow.

The other new sensation was more difficult to pinpoint. He had no fear or anxiety at all, but it was more than just the absence of the internal conflict – he truly felt a sense of peace and tranquility. More than that: he felt calm and serene, and knew in the very fiber of his being that everything was exactly as it was supposed to be at this point in time. He knew there was a design, that there was a purpose and meaning to life. His thoughts turned towards his Creator, and where once dwelt fear and shame and loathing he discovered acceptance and forgiveness and love - all this was now welling up within his heart.

They came to a place where the river slowed down and flowed around a bend. A short way downstream the riverbanks widened and the wildflowers which seemed to be everywhere in bloom reached almost to the water's edge. She placed Jeremiah on the shore and then turned back around to face him.

Her eyes were the crystal blue of the water and seemed to penetrate right to his heart. She floated there gracefully before his eyes, shimmering in the afternoon sun. He felt that she was respecting his silence, and knew that the first move toward dialogue would be his.

"Where do we go from here?" he asked, tears welling up in his eyes.

She smiled like nothing he had ever seen before; it was both sad and joyful at the same time, and it seemed to empathize completely with the struggle he was going through. "I am so glad you asked. Would you like to learn my native tongue?"

Jeremiah looked at her quizzically. "You could really teach me how to speak the language of the river?"

"Absolutely. The river, the stream, the babbling brook – all different dialects, but the same language."

"How would you teach me?"

"Look to your staff, Jeremiah."

Among the ornate runes, next to the word 'Gratitude" he found a new word was decipherable: "TRUST".

"Can you trust me, my friend?" Shannon seemed eager to share her secrets.

"Yes, I think I can. What must I do to learn?"

"You must become one with the water."

"Um…how does one become one with the water?" He thought that sounded awful silly once he had said it.

Shannon laughed. "Lay down your staff in the flowers, you will not need it for this part of the journey. I will see that it is returned to you later."

Jeremiah did as he was instructed.

"Now take this elixir of living water, and we will be on our way."

Shannon held out her hand and in the middle of her palm there was a small ball of perfectly blue water - the deepest, richest blue he had ever seen. He lifted it out of her hand, amazed at the way it kept its shape in his own palm while his fingers passed right through it. He placed it in his mouth and felt himself slip right into the river, and almost immediately he was traveling downstream with Shannon at his side.

Chapter VIII

The Secret Language
of Water

Jeremiah could never quite explain the sensation of being a fluid creature. The best description that he was able to come up with was that it was like when you are really, really tired and you feel yourself sink into a sofa or bed as you drift off to sleep. That was hardly an adequate description, but it was the closest thing to the feeling of fluidity that he could relate.

He was astonished at his ability to move about in the water. Shannon stayed right by his side as he swirled back and forth, moved against the flow of the river, and dove underwater to find that he was actually able to breathe and explore the river from below.

"This is incredible!" Jeremiah exclaimed. He was thrilled to find that his voice had taken on the same melodious quality that Shannon's voice exhibited. He continued to swirl about and jump in and out of the water, undulating with the river's current.

"This is where our lesson truly begins, Jeremiah. I need for you to allow the sounds around you to fill your senses. I realize how exciting it must be for you to have left the confines of your fleshly body and to flow with the river, but I need you to let go of all your expectations and truly just be present to the moment." Here she began to sing Jeremiah a water song:

Transcendence is that which we seek
when what we are is not enough
adherence to our Maker's heart
will keep us strong when seas get rough

The water takes the downward path
abandoning itself complete
Hear it bubble! Hear it laugh!
what joy! surrender sounds so sweet

Over hill and through the country
bending, winding, twisting round
Acquiescing to its calling
to always seek the lowest ground.

Lose yourself within the current
the living waters wash anew
Dare to be more than you hoped for
and you will see those hopes come true.

Jeremiah was taking in the rhythmic pulsing of the song and found that he and Shannon had begun swimming almost synchronously. They were headed for a section of fast moving water which rolled around and over some rather large rocks. He looked away from the rapids to find Shannon smiling serenely at him.

"Are you ready to face the rough waters, my friend?"

Jeremiah was surprised that he felt no fear as he looked back towards the rapidly changing river. "I am glad that we are in this together," he laughed.

Shannon joined her liquid hand to his. "Come, let us venture forth together. Remember, Jeremiah, you are never alone. Never trust appearances, always go with your heart's guidance."

The two of them rode over the crest of a small waterfall and were soon traveling downstream over rocks and under logs, round small eddies and riding around sharp corners, moving faster and faster. He could hardly tell whether he was under or over the water, or whether he was looking at the sky or the stream; he rolled and flowed with the river in joyful abandon until they came to a place where the river widened and slowed down.

"You see Jeremiah, you were not injured on the rapids because you have become a creature who can accept that which comes along, and surrender to your changing environment. Is the lesson clear?"

"I believe so," Jeremiah returned. "Is there more to come? I rather like being liquid, I believe that I could stay this way forever, if it were possible."

Shannon smiled and shook her head. "We were each made in our own fashion for a purpose. The greater good is for us to use our individual gifts to help one another. That is how we grow towards perfection, when we realize that we are all children of the same Maker despite all our apparent differences."

Here Shannon let go of his hand and raised both her hands towards the sun. She began to shimmer and grow; the colors of the sun made her appear to wear a resplendent garment. Jeremiah watched in speechless awe as she grew thinner and more drawn out. Her body began to separate into droplets, which in turn sparkled like diamonds as they began to separate, performing some type of elaborate dance above the surface of the water. They swirled faster and faster, weaving in and out of one another until the dance reached a crescendo of color and sound, the sound of many rushing waters congregating together in one body.

"Jeremiah, remember to follow your heart and not be deceived by appearances. You are on a great journey; you are greatly loved and capable of great love yourself. We will meet again, I promise."

With those words the entire dancing, swirling, spinning kaleidoscope was transformed into vapor. The mist settled on Jeremiah, and he regained his physical body. He swam to the edge of the river, climbed to the top of the banking, and promptly fell asleep in the wildflowers.

Chapter IX

Sacrifice Beneath the Stars

Jeremiah woke beneath the stars. He had no idea how long he had been asleep, there was no moon in the sky and everything around him was quiet as a tomb. As he lay there gazing at the stars, a feeling of awe and wonder crept over him.

His thoughts returned to Shannon, and the way in which she had vanished from his sight. He retained such a feeling of gratitude for their time together, and although it was short it seemed to Jeremiah that he had never felt such a kinship with another living creature.

The night was warm, and there were fireflies dancing over his head. They appeared to move in patterns, their movements curiously juxtaposed against the stars in the background. He became transfixed as the dance became more intricate, and he lost sight of which were the stars and which were the fireflies. He felt as if something were drawing him upwards, the heavens seemed to be close enough to touch. His breathing slowed and he began to feel as if he were floating above the ground.

He sat up quickly, his heart beating fast with fear. The feeling of weightlessness quickly disappeared and he found that he was still sitting among the flowers of the field. He would have liked to let go of his inhibitions and float out towards the stars, but something inside told him that he might not find his way back. In any case, he was certain that floating among the stars was not a part of his journey.

He stood up and surveyed his surroundings. He could not be certain how far he and Shannon had traveled downriver. Cassandra and Gwendolen had a way of finding him wherever he was, and he was certain that when the time was right they would reappear. In the meantime he decided that he should continue to follow the river, as there were no other discernable landmarks.

Jeremiah began walking along the bank of the river thinking what a shame it was that his staff was so far upstream, when he stubbed his toe on something hard. He reached down to find his staff right at his feet.

"That's strange, how did this get down here?" Jeremiah thought to himself. "It just doesn't make sense."

Just then he heard the mournful cry of the raven passing by overhead. His thoughts turned back to the last time he saw the raven, when he was standing at the top of the precipice with Gwendolen. "Unbelievable, he must have finished bearing my burden to the west and returned to help me. I wonder if Bertram sent him."

He smiled as he took the staff in his hands and looked at the engravings on the side. A new word was visible, glowing with a strange luminescence in the dark: "SACRIFICE".

Jeremiah nodded his head in recognition. As he continued his trek downstream, he recalled the time his grandfather tried to explain love to him when he was a child.

They had been sitting out on the front porch swing gazing at the evening stars, Jeremiah was sitting close to his grandfather and squeezed his hand and told him how much he loved him.

His grampa returned the squeeze and smiled down at him. "Jeremiah, love isn't just a feeling you know."

"Well, what is it grampa?"

"The most important thing to know about love is that it isn't a thing at all. Love is a verb, it is caring in action. When our Lord said to love God with everything you've got and to love your neighbor as yourself, he wasn't talking about feeling all warm and gushy inside. He meant to show your love by what you do."

"How do I do that, grampa?"

"At your age, you do that just by asking these questions. It gets harder as you get older. The one thing to remember is that the desire to please God is in itself pleasing to God. Your wanting to love Him right now is exactly the same as loving Him. He looks at the heart, I think the best way of explaining the difference between the world's love and God's love would be sacrifice."

"You mean like when Jesus died on the cross?"

"Yes, Jeremiah. That is the ultimate example. We are called to lay down our lives for each other, but in a different way."

"I don't understand grampa…"

"Well, maybe I can explain it this way. If you were crossing the street, and I saw a car coming straight at you that would surely hit you, I would make sure that I dove in front of the car to push you away, even though it would probably mean the end of my life. That is one kind of sacrifice."

Jeremiah's face lit up with understanding. "Oh, I see. You would give your life to save mine." A cloud came across his countenance. "I hope that never happens, grampa."

He put both arms around Jeremiah and pulled him close. "I hope not either."

After a short period of silence, Jeremiah asked his grampa "Are there other kinds of sacrifice that aren't so scary?"

His grampa smiled down at him. "Why yes there are. There are the daily sacrifices that we make which are just as pleasing to the Creator. When we open the door and let someone go ahead of us because they are carrying a heavy package, when we give our time to a friend in need, when we offer a smile to a homeless person who most people pass by without a glance; these are all ways of giving from the heart."

"But all those things make you feel good inside…"

Grampa laughed, "That is very true. And those are all things that you would do naturally as a young boy. As you get older, you will find life will get busier, and it will become harder to express that selfless giving."

"I hope I never forget grampa."

"It is written on your heart, Jeremiah. You are never too old to return to that."

Jeremiah smiled wistfully at the thought of his grampa as he walked along the banks of the river. He had always been so kind, so patient. He had not been able to enter into another close relationship after his grampa died. He had shut down completely, not allowing anyone in. No one at all…

His thoughts were interrupted by the appearance of a campfire off in the distance. As he drew closer, he could see that it was a large bonfire, and there were several large figures around it. He had a tingling sensation of danger, and so he crept off to the cover of some large rocks at the base of a cliff.

He made his way close enough to the campfire to observe what was happening. In the center of a clearing was the bonfire. There was a creature with a bag over its head that was tied to a stake close to where Jeremiah was hiding. Around the campfire there were three shadowy figures arguing.

"He is mine, I tell you," the first figure demanded.

"Not so, Faer," the second one called out. "I hunted him as well as you. Without my passion you would not have caught him."

Faer sneered, "It was I who set the trap, Hete. Without me you would have nothing."

At this point, the third figure rose up off the ground. He was enormous and the other two seemed to shrink back from his imposing figure.

"If I had not filled his senses, he would never have fallen prey to you two. Count yourselves fortunate that I have decided to allow you to share in the spoils."

The first two figures bowed low to the ground and said in unison, "Yes, my lord Pryde. We understand."

Jeremiah spied a fourth figure who sat apart from the first three. They appeared to take no notice of its presence.

"Let us continue with the ritual then," Pryde continued. The three of them rose and began a strange rhythmic chanting as they danced around the fire. Jeremiah could see that the figures were not human at all; they were more like dark wraiths which moved with a strange fluidity around the fire.

Jeremiah slipped carefully down the rock behind the captive form and whispered, "Don't make a sound. I'm going to get you out of here."

The figure made no movement at all, Jeremiah wondered if he was drugged or passed out. This creature was not tied to the stake, he was chained there. Jeremiah wondered how he would loose his bonds.

The fourth figure got up off the ground and walked right by the dancing wraiths. They took no notice of its crossing, continuing their strange ritual. Jeremiah felt strangely calm as this hooded figure came straight for the prisoner.

"Jeremiah..." the figure spoke his name in a voice like he had never heard before. It was full of power and authority, he felt compelled to obey out of sheer love. It filled him with a sense of courage and strength. As he stood up, the prisoner stood up at the same time.

The three wraiths around the fire stopped their dancing and chanting and began to howl like animals. They rose up to their full heights and attempted to spring upon the hooded figure, their absolute blackness filling the air and blotting out the stars overhead.

Jeremiah jumped in front of the prisoner with his staff held high, prepared to fend them off with his life, if need be. The hooded figure turned towards the approaching specters, held out his hand and spoke one word of command:

"BEGONE!"

With that word he threw back his hood, and light blazed forth transforming the night into the brilliance of the sun.

Chapter X

The Way to the Summit

Jeremiah was stunned by the sudden dazzling light all around him, it seemed to come from everywhere and nowhere, all was light and there was no shadow, nothing to form a shadow anywhere within view. The night was gone, the wraiths were gone, the man who rescued them – there was nothing but light.

Jeremiah looked down at his own body and gasped, it appeared as if he were made entirely of light. He could not distinguish his own features from the brilliance which surrounded him, engulfed him; it seemed to come from within him and from all about him.

He felt weightless, as if something incredibly good was filling him from the inside out. His body relaxed, and everything seemed to feel perfectly in place. All the anxieties and fears that had crippled him for years just seemed to disappear.

There was only one thing that seemed appropriate to do to express the way he was feeling, this utter relief and thankfulness. Jeremiah began to laugh.

At first, it was the laughter of relief, like when a great storm finally passes over. The gentle laughter began to grow louder, and the more he laughed the more he wanted to laugh, until it became a genuine belly laugh, and tears were flowing down his face and he was on the ground, holding both sides for fear that he might explode.

After some time, Jeremiah regained his composure and opened his eyes. The all pervading light had become the normal light of the new day. Exhausted and panting from the long overdue release of emotion, he felt thirsty and walked over to the river to slake his thirst.

He knelt down and began to drink from the stream. The more he drank, the more he wanted to keep on drinking. It was invigorating, he felt like he was becoming more and more alive with each draught.

When he had finally satisfied his thirst, he stood and turned around to survey the terrain. He was at the base of a mountain, possibly the same mountain that Gwendolen had pointed out earlier.

He walked over to the stake where the prisoner had been bound and found his staff and flute lying next to the empty shackles. Now he knew that he indeed had been the prisoner, and his Rescuer had done more than simply set him free – he had restored both strength and joy to this journey.

The words on the side of his flute caught his eye. He knelt down to examine the new word there among the ancient hieroglyphs: SURRENDER. This was the same word that the raven had whispered in his ear before he went to face the dragon in the fire. The very same word he had used in quite a different manner as a battle cry in his youth: NEVER SURRENDER! He smiled and nodded his head; he now had a measure of understanding of what true humility is, and Who it is that he should be surrendering to.

As he stood up and looked down the range at the base of the mountain, he could see something sparkling off in the distance among the rocks, almost like a light reflecting off a mirror. He hurried over to discover the source of the light. When he arrived there he found no light source, but he did discover a foot path up the mountainside.

The way began easy enough; the path was wide and well worn from the passage of time. There were flowers and tall grasses along the path, butterflies flitted here and there, and Jeremiah whistled as he wended his way upwards.

After a time he came to a large open area, with a small mountain tarn in the center. He was glad at the sight of it, for he had been walking for quite some time at this point and had grown thirsty. As soon as he knelt down and began to drink, that same feeling of heightened awareness that he had experienced in Bertram's cottage stole upon him. He stood up and looked farther up the trail, again the sparkling that he had seen at the base of the mountain occurred off in the distance. This time it appeared roughly human in shape, and beckoned him to follow.

By the time he had walked around the small lake and reached the area that the figure had been, it had eluded him. Up ahead in the distance he could hear the sound of running water. He hurried around the bend and discovered a series of small waterfalls coming out of the side of the mountain. There was a rough hewn stairway of stone running alongside the water, just off the mountain trail.

Jeremiah walked up the steps leading to the cave, and as he drew closer he noticed that there were vines that covered the opening and trailed their long stems into the water. It appeared as if they were performing some elaborate dance to the music of the water. The flowers on the other side of the path seemed to sway with the rhythm; everything around him seemed so alive and vibrant. The entire scene stirred something in Jeremiah, and he yearned to join in this natural symphony.

Just when he thought his heart would burst with ecstasy, he heard another melody coming from the mountain. This music came from behind those swaying vines and seemed to envelop him in a shroud of peace, the melody blending in with the natural cadence surrounding him. He felt drawn to this new music like nothing had ever attracted him before.

He continued up the walkway as if in a waking dream, all his senses tingled with anticipation at the thought of what lay behind the curtain of vines blocking the entrance to the mountain. The steps ended at the top of the first cascading waterfall, and as he brushed the vines aside to look within he saw a small ledge, just large enough to walk on, which ran next to the inner stream.

Once Jeremiah stepped inside the mountain, the music became more defined. He felt like it was all around him and within him at the same time. It was unlike any earthly music he had ever heard: it was beyond words, beyond instruments. It was the sweetest, purest, most harmonious sound that could be imagined. Jeremiah breathed it in like life.

As he came around the corner, he viewed a great open cavern with an enormous stone fountain directly in the center. The water was gushing out of the top, as if it were leaping for joy out of the depths of the mountain and springing to life. This water filled the lower part of the basin, which in turn overflowed into the stream that issued forth from the cave entrance.

Jeremiah yearned to jump in the fountain, to immerse himself in these waters which carried the very essence of life. Somehow he knew that was not the right course, and he pulled himself out of his rapture and continued along the stone ledge until he came to another stone staircase at the back of the cavern. With one last longing look back at the glorious fountain, he continued on the path set before him up the rough hewn staircase.

The music began to fade, and his spirits sank. He wondered if he should run back down the staircase and return to the fountain. He paused for a time considering this, and again with much effort he resumed his upward climb.

He emerged from the top of the stone staircase into a large open area on the mountain which had the appearance of an outdoor amphitheatre with high rock walls all around. In the very center of the clearing there was an old stone well with long marble benches on either side of it. On one of the benches was the sparkling figure that had beckoned him from the base of the mountain.

As Jeremiah approached, he could see that the figure was definitely human in shape, but like Shannon was not human in form. He could not discern what substance this creature was made of; there was something similar to the light from a prism, but there was also a sense of colors beyond the normal spectrum. The figure seemed to be sitting on the bench, but there was also the suggestion of movement within the confines of the body.

Jeremiah reached the well and found that there was already a bucket full of water with two cups set beside it. He looked into the bucket and discovered that the water within seemed to be vibrant with life, just like the figure which sat on the bench with its arm extended. Although it had no discernable facial features the figure conveyed an unmistakable aura of goodness and tranquility. Jeremiah picked up the two cups, handed one to the stranger, and brought the other to his lips.

The liquid felt so calming going down, he found it hard to believe that it was only water that he was drinking.

"Hello Jeremiah, you are looking well these days."

Jeremiah dropped the cup and stood staring dumbly at the vision which had appeared before him. In place of the sparkling silhouette now sat his long deceased grandfather.

Chapter XI

Catharsis

Jeremiah slumped down onto the stone bench opposite his grandfather, burying his face in his hands.

His grandfather smiled and seemed to read his thoughts. "No, Jeremiah, you aren't dead. And yes, this is really me. Go ahead, reach out and touch me."

Jeremiah looked up at his grandfather, and yes, it certainly looked like him – and yet, it was as if the person standing before him was more than just the man he knew and loved in his youth. He reached for him, and his grampa pulled him into an embrace. For the moment, all his doubts and anxiety and confusion melted away in that embrace.

"Come, Jeremiah, let us walk awhile."

Jeremiah picked up his staff off the ground and they walked to the far side of the amphitheater where the upwards path continued on.

"Grampa, if I am not dead, then how is it I am walking beside you now? You left the world when I was a young boy." Jeremiah restrained a catch in his throat. "I missed you terribly."

His grampa put an arm around his shoulders. "It wasn't your fault Jeremiah."

Everything came rushing back at Jeremiah. "It *was* my fault. It was all my fault. If I hadn't asked you to go out...If I could have just waited until the morning...You would have...you wouldn't have..."

"Jeremiah," he spoke softer now, "it wasn't your fault."

"They said it was my fault. They said you were always doting on me, that if I hadn't asked you to go you would never have crashed the car. I did it. I MADE YOU GO. I KILLED YOU! I KILLED YOU!!"

Jeremiah broke down and began sobbing uncontrollably. His grampa put his arms around him again, whispered again in his ear: "Jeremiah, it wasn't your fault. Life happens. God is there to bring us through."

Jeremiah broke away from his embrace. His eyes flashed anger. "GOD? Where was God when I needed him? Where was he in school? Where was he in my home? Why did he let you die? Why didn't he help me? Why did he leave me all alone to fall on my face time and again?" The anger drained out of him and he sat down on a rock. "I'm sorry grampa. I'm so sorry..."

Grampa sat down on the rock next to Jeremiah and took his hand. "No need to be sorry, son. This is all very sudden and your feelings have been buried for a very long time. I understand." He stood up and gently raised Jeremiah by the hand. "Shall we continue towards the summit?"

Jeremiah nodded and they resumed their trek towards the top.

"Jeremiah, do you remember our coffee table talks?"

Jeremiah laughed. "I always liked them, because they came with coffee cake."

Grampa chuckled. "That's right. Do you remember the talks we had about life as a journey?"

Jeremiah's skin tingled as if it were electric. "Yes, I do. It seems so long ago now, but I had this dream about a place where everything just seemed to make sense. I had never experienced anything as real as the place that I visited in that dream. I remember waking from that dream and trying to find a pen and by the time I found it I forgot most of the details. The thing that stayed with me was that sense of home, of belonging. I thought the best way to try and figure out what it all meant was to catch a Greyhound bus back to where I grew up. I remember getting on the bus…I remember meeting Cassandra…"

Grampa gave him a pat on the back. "Yes, Cassandra is very special."

Jeremiah gave his grandfather an incredulous look.

"Oh yes, Jeremiah, I know Cassandra and Gwendolen. I have been to the house of Bertram, and have swum in the living waters with Shannon. I have had my own journey, you know."

"Where am I grampa? What does all this mean?"

"This is your journey, Jeremiah. It will mean something different for you than it did for me. You should know that you are never alone, even when it appears so. Do you have a flute in your pocket?"

Jeremiah pulled out the flute.

"Why don't I play us a tune while we walk, and you can relate your journey to me?"

For the rest of the trip up the mountain, Jeremiah told the tale of his adventures in this strange land while his grandfather played music on the flute. The music seemed to ebb and flow with the various parts of his journey, weaving a tapestry out of the events which Jeremiah had recently experienced.

When grampa finished playing the flute, they both stopped and looked at each other for a long time. Jeremiah had the feeling that his life made sense for the first time, he knew that he was not alone, had never been alone or abandoned. And although he was still not certain where he was headed, he was no longer anxious or afraid. He sensed that the time had come for he and his grandfather to part again.

"Thank you, grampa."

He smiled at Jeremiah in return. "This is not goodbye, only farewell for now. This last leg of the journey is yours alone."

Jeremiah reached out and pulled his grandfather into a hug. "I love you grampa."

"I love you too, Jeremiah."

Their embrace became a melting together, and soon Jeremiah was standing alone on the path, the flute in his pocket and the staff in his hand.

Chapter XII

The Riddle

He came around the bend in the path to discover that he had reached a lookout point on the mountain. Before him lay the entire country that he had traveled: from the distant cottage at the forest's edge, to the range of mountains that he was now standing on. It was breathtaking.

After a short rest while he pondered the significance of his journey, he continued the path up a very rough and steep section of the mountain to reach the apex. At the top was a large clearing, and his view of the land was now completely unobstructed. The great Ocean stretched out before him as far as his eye could see. In the center of the clearing there was an area with a large smooth black stone, which stood like a massive monument reaching for the sky.

Jeremiah approached the stone, and found these words in gold lettering emblazoned on its face:

I am always there
yet cannot be seen
Was discovered by man

but have always been
I cannot be harnessed
though many have tried
I can cause great oceans
to become dried
I can haunt you till
the day you die
Tell me now
who am I?

A riddle? Jeremiah thought that was particularly odd, especially at this point in his journey. He wondered what it signified, and how he would solve it.

He walked over to the side of the clearing which faced the ocean, and gazed down the almost sheer face of this side of the mountain. He realized that the whole way up had been a trip with only an interior view; he had not once had a glimpse of the sea which now lay before him. It seemed like his journey had reached its climax with no way to go and an enigmatic ending. And yet, he did not feel confused or hopeless at all. He felt as if this was exactly where he was supposed to be at this point in time, doing exactly what he was supposed to do in this moment.

Quite suddenly, he felt tired. Really tired. He sat down on a large rock at the edge of the precipice and allowed the feeling to just wash over him. He had lost his fear, his anxiety, and his hopelessness – those bogeymen which had been with him as long as he could remember. The feeling which was bathing him at the top of the mountain was peace. Honest, pure, and otherworldly peace. Something he had never experienced before, and he knew right then and there that he was created to be more than he had ever known or understood.

He laid on that rock flat on his back and stared up at the bright blue sky. He thought of the mentors that had greeted him on the journey. Bertram, the old healer in the cottage who was so kind to him. Cassandra, who always had a word of wisdom to help him find his the next step on the path. Gwendolen, who radiated a joy so full that it could not help but be contagious. Shannon, who taught him the importance of letting go and embracing change. The mysterious hooded figure that had set him free at the base of the mountain. And his grandfather – they all had one thing in common. They all encouraged him to face the things that had wounded him. They all moved him towards healing. They helped him to reach the summit of his journey. It just took time.

Time heals all wounds.

God heals all wounds in time, his grampa would say.

Time.

Time…

Time!

The riddle's answer was time.

"Yes, it is time, Jeremiah. You have learned well."

Jeremiah sat up and quickly turned around. Next to where the monument stood were his companions: Bertram, Cassandra, Gwendolen, and Shannon were all there...and yet, they were less substantial then when he had last seen them. They appeared as ethereal bodies up here at the top of the mountain.

Standing next to them was the figure who had spoken. "Your friends have come to bid you farewell."

The figure was a tall man, shrouded in a midnight blue robe. He appeared to be very old, and yet his eyes sparkled with vibrant life. In his right hand was a staff of pure gold, with a dark glass orb attached to the top. The raven which had borne Jeremiah's burden across the great sea was seated on his left shoulder.

Bertram was the first to step forward. "Farewell, Jeremiah. Remember the lesson you learned in my cottage. Share it with others."

"I will, Bertram. Thank you for your kindness."

They embraced, and in the same way that his grandfather had become a part of him, so also did Jeremiah come out of that embrace standing alone but more fully whole. He did notice that the orb at the top of the stranger's staff glowed a little brighter.

"You have learned my language, Jeremiah, teach others the same."

"I will, Shannon. Thank you for your gifts of acceptance and surrender."

As they embraced, Jeremiah once again felt that extraordinary sense of being something more than just confined to this earthly shell.

"You will always find me when you look for me, Jeremiah. I am on the other side of every trial and tribulation you encounter. Be sure and tell others about me, that they too may find strength for the journey."

Jeremiah laughed. "I consider it pure joy to know you, Gwendolen. Thank you for the gift of laughter."

In their farewell, he could feel the warmth of her presence settling deep inside his being. It was like a cup of hot cocoa on a cold winter's day.

He looked over to Cassandra, and as she walked towards him she began as the child he had met on the bus, and aged with each step, until she stood before him a wise old woman of indeterminate age, fashioned in timeless beauty.

"Jeremiah, you have learned to walk in beauty and truth. You have faced your fears and learned grace. It was I who drew you here, to meet the One who had the power to heal you. And so He has. May you find the Great Healer in every one you meet."

"I ...I love you Cassandra..." Jeremiah was too overcome with emotion to continue.

"Yes, my child. You do love. That is the true gift that healing brings." She lifted his head so that their eyes met. "You have become love. Share the gift of yourself with those you meet. And know that you are indeed loved in return."

When Cassandra put her arms around him, he realized that what she was saying was true. He no longer felt unworthy. He felt at home in his body, at peace with himself, and unafraid of the future. In her eyes he had seen himself, and he knew he belonged.

In a flash of light, she was gone from his sight.

Jeremiah looked over at the robed man still standing across the way. The globe at the top of his staff was now a dazzling light, radiating brighter than the daylight around him. The raven looked from Jeremiah to the stranger, and then hopped into the globe, at which point it ceased its glowing.

"That was very nicely done, my son."

"Do I know you, sir?"

"I am the Keeper of the Memories, Jeremiah. Very soon you will not remember me at all, but I will not be offended in the least. I prefer the anonymity. Your time here is nearly at an end."

"I don't understand. Where am I going from here? Will I be traveling to the Land over the Sea?"

"This is not your time to cross the Great Sea. You have received a healing, and with that healing comes a great responsibility. You are to take that back to the wasteland to teach others."

"I don't know the way, sir."

"That is why I have come. I am here to facilitate your transition."

Jeremiah resisted the impulse to ask more questions. He felt calmness come over him again, and waited for the Keeper to explain further.

"Your staff and your flute, bring them to me."

Jeremiah did as he was beckoned. The Keeper asked him, "What do you see there engraved upon the flute?"

Jeremiah held the flute aloft. "There are still many of the runes I cannot read, but the ones that I have learned are: Forgiveness, Joy, and Surrender."

"And upon the staff, which words have appeared out of the inscriptions that you found there?"

Jeremiah lifted the staff up so that they could both see the lettering upon it. "Gratitude, Trust, and Sacrifice were made manifest there, sir."

"Yes, very good. Exactly as it should be." Here the Keeper produced a small gold box from inside the folds of his robe. He threw it at the ground and immediately a fire rose up nearly as tall as the Keeper himself.

Very softly, but very firmly he said, "Jeremiah, you must place them in the fire."

Something rose up inside Jeremiah that made him want to shout 'NO!' at the thought of destroying the tools which had helped him so much along the way. He turned his eyes away from the Keeper and looked out towards the Sea.

"Jeremiah, you must place them in the fire."

What would he have left? His friends were gone, he was left alone at the top of the mountain with a mysterious stranger, and he had no idea where he was going next. How could he let go of the only sure things he knew?

"Jeremiah, you must place them in the fire."

The Keeper's voice was an odd mixture of authority and supplication. He looked back towards the sage and discovered that his arms were held wide over the fire, the staff raised and a strange far away look on his face.

Jeremiah looked again at his staff and flute. What use were Sacrifice and Surrender if they were only words which served their purpose and did not become a living, active part of him?

Jeremiah tossed both items into the flames. He looked across the blaze and met the Keeper's eyes. The far away look was gone and his face broke into a grin.

"Are you ready to go home, Jeremiah?"

The word home resonated somewhere deep inside him. He nodded his agreement.

"You have done well, my son. You will learn the meaning of the rest of the carvings soon enough." The Keeper lifted his staff over his head, and with one word brought it crashing into the center of the conflagration:

"HOME!"

The fire shot straight up into the sky for a moment and then came crashing down. It consumed the Keeper, the Mountain, the Land, and Jeremiah himself.

Chapter XIII

A New Beginning

Forgiveness breathes the freshest air
unchained from hatred, free from care

Joy will follow every sorrow
when we let go of tomorrow

Surrender leaves the ego dead
allows the Spirit to clear the head

Gratitude in place of complaint
will lift the heart, remove restraint

Trust will come in its own time
when we reach for the Divine

Sacrifice, the tool we acquire
to rescue others from hellfire.

Jeremiah felt like he was a floating, disembodied entity. He could not see or feel anything of his body. The song came to him in unbroken, melodic couplets. It was in harmony with what he was experiencing, and brought him an enormous sense of peace. All around him drifted what appeared to be wisps of clouds and everything was bathed in a soft light. He also felt as if he had completed a momentous task, and was now able to see and hear clearly for the first time.

"Thank you, God."

The words came from within him and without him, reverberating in that peaceful stillness, filling all his senses with an overwhelming awareness of Something greater than himself, Something infinitely larger and more powerful - Something wholly and unreservedly good. In that tiny moment in time, in the space of an instant, he completely and utterly abandoned himself into the Hands of that Unknown God, into the Arms of the Creator, to the Silent Fourth figure who had set him free by the foot of the mountain.

"I surrender."

He heard a sound in the distance which he thought might be thunder, and the clouds around him began to darken and move quickly past. He began to feel heavier, although he could still see nothing of his body he began to feel its weight pulling him downwards.

He felt no fear, no trepidation, no anxiety. He continued to plunge faster and faster, he felt the weight of his body but still could not see his physical form. He had taken the last leap of faith, and was determined to trust with everything that he had that the One who had led him this far would not let go of him.

He hit bottom. It was like smashing into a moving bus. Everything hurt. He could not move any part of his body. Everything was dark. There was no sound. All was still, unmoving, expectant. Then he heard a beep.

Then another beep.

He lay in the dark, disoriented - groping in his mind for understanding.

Another beep.

The sounds of movement, something making a swishing or shuffling sound.

Silence.

The darkness began to recede. He could hear himself breathing. The blackness turned to a dark reddish color, then a light tan. His eyes shot open and he was staring at the fluorescent bulbs of a hospital room.

"Jeremiah, you're back! You're okay!! I knew you would come back, I just knew it."

He could hear the warmth of love and concern in that voice, and it helped bring him back around. "Anastasia…?"

She took his hand and stood up so that he could see her face. "I am so sorry that we fought. I should have understood how important it was for you to follow your heart and go back to your hometown. I was just so afraid. You seemed so distant. And then I got the call that your bus had been in an accident…"

"An accident?" Jeremiah whispered.

"All I could think of was the angry last words I spoke as you left…"

"The Greyhound bus…"

Anastasia continued. "And you've been in this coma now for 2 weeks, and the doctors didn't know whether you were going to make it…"

Jeremiah turned his head slightly so that he could look Anastasia in the eye. "Stacia, I feel like I've been in a coma all my life. Thank you for being so patient."

She began to cry and kiss him and squeeze his hand, and although it hurt like crazy he smiled at her and knew that everything was going to be okay.

Epilogue

In each of us is a hope that the journey will lead us Home. That we will find that place where we truly belong, where everything falls into place and all of our questions are laid to rest. Where our hearts no longer ache, our bodies no longer hurt, our minds no longer race, and our spirits are at peace.

The man who experienced the dream of what life was meant to be like learned to live the life that he was meant to lead. He learned that he was not alone on his journey, and that the journey was meant to be shared.

Cast of Characters

JEREMIAH
From the Hebrew name Yirmeyahu, which means "YAHWEH has uplifted".

CASSANDRA
From the Greek Kassandra, which means "shining upon man".

BERTRAM
Means "bright raven", derived from the Germanic element beraht "bright" combined with hramn "raven".

THE RAVEN
In Australia the Raven is known as a bird of sorrows. It is believed that he takes the sadness from humanity and flies it away, his mournful cry telling of the burden that he carries so that people may have relief.

GWENDOLEN
Means "white ring", derived from the Welsh elements gwen "white, fair, blessed" and dolen "ring".

SHANNON
From the name of the Shannon River, the longest river in Ireland. It is composed of the Gaelic elements sean "old, wise" and abhann "river".

ANASTASIA
Feminine form of the Greek name "Anastasuis", which is the Latinized form of the Greek name "Anastaios" which means "resurrection" (asastasis).

All name etymologies thanks to Mike at Behindthename.com